It was spring once again—time for Casey Jr., the circus train, to take the circus to town.

The cars were loaded with animals, clowns and acrobats. Casey Jr. was anxious to get started. "All aboard! Let's go!"

The train was filled with new baby animals. There were baby hippos and baby zebras, baby giraffes and baby lions. In the elephant car, Mrs. Jumbo had just received her own beautiful little baby. She called him Jumbo Jr.

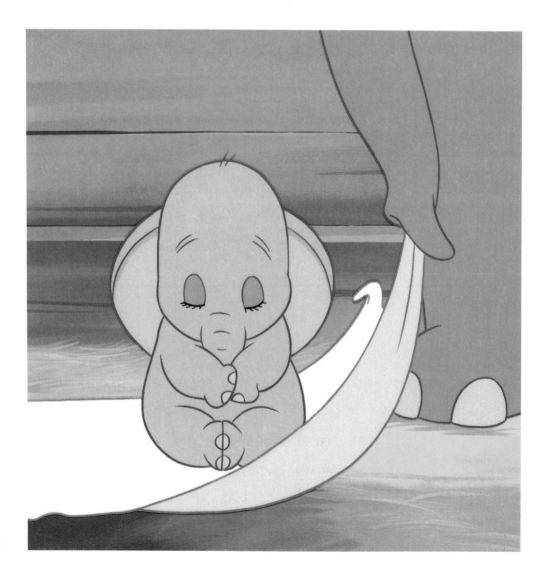

This was a proud, proud day for all the elephants. Mrs. Jumbo's friends fussed and cooed over the cute baby. Suddenly, the little elephant sneezed. "AH-CHOO!" What a surprise! Out flapped the largest ears anyone had ever seen—even on an elephant!

"He looks like a clown," laughed one elephant. "Little Jumbo? He looks more like little Dumbo!"

Little Dumbo was teary-eyed as he looked at his ears. It was true; they were big.

But Mrs. Jumbo didn't care. She cuddled little Dumbo in her trunk and gently rocked him to sleep.

Casey Jr. stopped at a small town, and all the animals and circus performers paraded down the main street. The crowd cheered the monkeys and the clowns and the circus band. But their cheers turned to laughter when they saw the little elephant with the big, big ears.

5

The people followed the parade to the circus grounds.
A group of rowdy boys saw little Dumbo and began to
tease him. One of the boys even tugged on Dumbo's
ears. "Look at those sailboat ears!"

Mrs. Jumbo was furious. She turned the boy over and gave him a good spanking with her trunk. Then she sprayed water over all the boys. The crowd panicked. "Wild elephant!" they shouted as they ran for the tent exits.

The ringmaster saw all the people running from the tent and heard their cries. He thought Mrs. Jumbo had really gone wild, so he locked her up in a prison wagon. Poor little Dumbo was left all alone.

DANGER

MAD ELEPHANT

DANGER KEEP OUT

To make matters worse, the ringmaster dressed the little elephant in a silly costume and put him in a clown act. Dumbo had to jump from the top of a building into a net held by the clowns. Every time, he would crash through the net and land in a tub of soapsuds. Everyone thought the act was very funny—everyone except Dumbo.

Poor Dumbo! None of the other elephants would even talk to him. Then Timothy, the circus mouse, noticed the little elephant one day, walking by himself. "There he goes, without a friend in the world. I'll fix that!

"Hey, Dumbo," said Timothy. "I'll be your friend. There's nothing wrong with your ears. Why don't we work them into an act? I'll make you famous. If you're the star of the show, no one will dare laugh at you, and they'll have to let your mother out of her prison wagon."

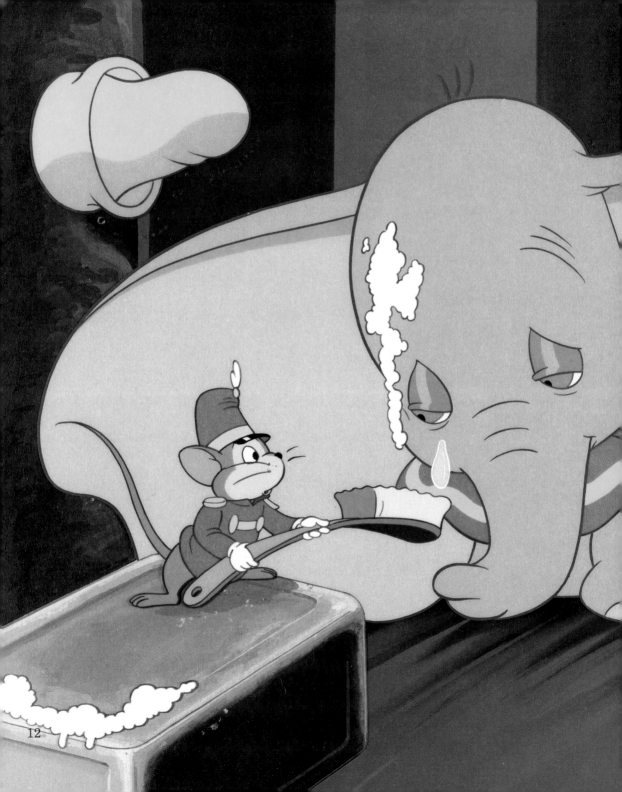

"Here! Let me have a look at those ears," said Timothy. Dumbo happily waved his ears so Timothy could see just how big they were.

"Ho, ho! They're colossal! Stupendous! But what can we do with them?"

Timothy thought and thought. "Say! Maybe you could leap through the air like the acrobats."

Dumbo tried, but he fell flat on his face.

"That won't work," said Timothy. "But we'll think of something. Don't be discouraged."

13

But Timothy himself had no idea what they were going to do. It seemed hopeless.

By now it was nighttime, so Timothy curled up in Dumbo's clown hat, and they both went to sleep.

And during the night, Dumbo had the strangest dream. He dreamed he could fly!

The next morning, Timothy was awakened by some laughing crows. "What are you birds doing down here? Why don't you go fly up a tree, where you belong?"

"What are we doing down here? Listen to him! You'd better look again, brother."

"What do you mean...uh-oh! Dumbo! Don't look now, but I think we're up a tree!"

It was true. Dumbo and Timothy were really out on a limb. Poor Dumbo was so startled that he lost his balance and fell right into a puddle of water.

The crows laughed and laughed. Timothy was
bewildered. "Dumbo, how'd we get up in that tree?"
 One of the crows chuckled. "Maybe you flew up!"
 "That's it, Dumbo! You flew! Ho, ho! Why didn't I
think of this before? Your ears! They're perfect wings!"
 "You're right about that!" laughed the crows.

Timothy was angry. "You should be ashamed, picking on Dumbo. His mother is locked up, and they've made him a clown, and everyone laughs at him."

The crows felt sorry. The largest one whispered to Timothy. "He has to believe he can fly. Tell him this magic feather will do the trick!"

Timothy took Dumbo to the edge of a tall cliff. "Okay, now, hold this magic feather and start flapping your ears!"

Dumbo flapped and flapped, and to everyone's surprise, he soared off the cliff!

"It worked, Dumbo!"

Dumbo and Timothy saved their surprise for the afternoon performance. Timothy perched on Dumbo's hat as they sat on top of the building, ready for the clown act.

"Okay, Dumbo! Got the magic feather? Good. Then take off!"

But when Dumbo jumped, he lost hold of the feather. Down they fell! "Flap your ears, Dumbo! That feather wasn't really magic. You can fly without it!"

Dumbo spread his great ears, and off he sailed. The crowd was astonished as the little elephant soared high above their heads. Timothy was overjoyed. "We did it! Dumbo, you're a sensation! A star!"

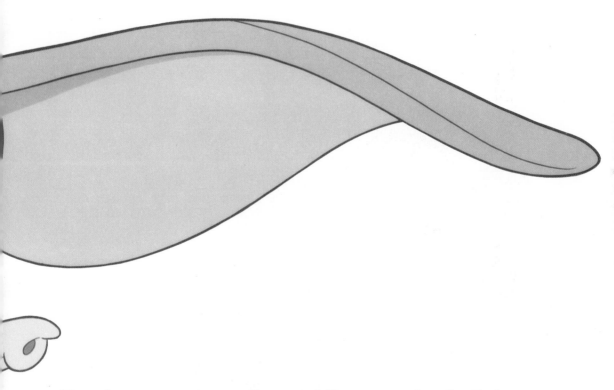

Dumbo was a star—the world's one and only flying elephant. The ringmaster released Dumbo's mother and gave her a special railroad car of her own.

And no one ever laughed at Dumbo's ears again.